for Finley & Avery- R.K.
for my Perfect Family- A.L.

special thanks to Miss Jill

This Book is PERFeCT!

By Ron Keres
Artwork by Arthur Lin

SCHOLASTIC

Oh, hello there.

I'm Finn the **FROG** and **THIS**, my friend, is the **CLEANEST** book you will ever see!

Some even say that it's **PERFECT**, but I don't really like to brag.

I know, I know. Most frogs are **SLIMY** and **DIRTY**. But not me. No way. You see, I am the tidiest frog you will ever meet.

I think you're going to be quite impressed with what you are about to see.

Now then, shall we begin?
Go on. Turn the page.

AHHHHH!

What is on your fingers?!
Are you eating **CHEESY PUFFS**
while reading **MY** book??

What are you thinking!?
You can't eat cheesy puffs
while reading this book! Wipe
your hands and put that
snack away **RIGHT NOW!!**

Whew, that's better. A little elbow grease goes a long way when keeping things neat, you know.

And after all, it could have been worse. It could have been—

GRAPE JUICE!

Are you kidding me?
Sticky, drippy grape juice
all over my **PERFECT** pages?

Listen, kid. If there is anything you've got to know in life, it's this: grape juice **ALWAYS** stains!

These pages are supposed to be white, not **PURPLE!** This is not good, kid.
Not Good!

DRAT! This mop is worthless against such a mess! First the fingerprints, now the grape juice. I swear, this day couldn't get any–

WHAT HAVE YOU DONE?!?

This is a nightmare. It has to be.
Any minute now I'm going to wake up and find out that there is not **GUM** stuck on my page!
It will be fine. Really.

Any . . . minute . . . now.
Wake up, Finn. Wake up **NOW!**

It's not working. I don't think
I'm dreaming.

Breathe, Finn, breathe.
There must be something I
can use to get that sticky
thing off my book?

MAYDAY! MAYDAY! This is not a drill.
I repeat, this is not a drill.
My page is **RIPPING!**

This is a disaster! I was so excited to show you my book, but now it is ruined forever!

Ugh. I just want this all to be over. Maybe you should just close the book and end my misery.

WAIT! Don't close the book. Do you see what I see? This mess is attracting flies! Don't you know those tiny troublemakers throw up every time they land?

YUCK! Even the thought of fly **BARF** on my book is making me queasy.

Shoo, fly! Shoo! Go away!

Oh, no. That useless fly just
landed on my book!
Think, Finn, think. How does
one get rid of flies??

Hmmm. I wonder if my vacuum
has a turbo mode for sucking up flies?

PEANUT

NO! Don't smash it, kid. Do you have any idea the kind of mess that would leave behind? I mean, all the guts and other oozy stuff that comes out of a fly? Not on **MY** book!

There's got to be another way.

Me? Why are you looking at me?
What do you expect me to do?!

Oooooh. Right.

AHH!!!
SLUURRPPP!!
PEANUT

Mmmmm! **DEE-LISH!** I almost forgot how good those things taste! You know, I still believe cleanliness is the best policy, but maybe this mess wasn't so terrible after all.

Come to think of it, without your help,
I never would have gotten these
tasty snacks! And besides, if I
can't live with the mess . . .

I can always turn the page!

SLUURRPPP!!
PERFECT!

Scholastic Australia
PO Box 579 Gosford NSW 2250
ABN 11 000 614 577
www.scholastic.com.au

Part of the Scholastic Group
Sydney • Auckland • New York • Toronto • London • Mexico City
• New Delhi • Hong Kong • Buenos Aires • Puerto Rico

First published by Buzzbook Press in 2022.
Published by Scholastic Australia in 2024.

Illustrations by Arthur Lin.

ISBN 978-1-76164-095-7

Printed in China by RR Donnelley.

Scholastic Australia's policy, in association with RR Donnelley, is to use papers that are renewable and made efficiently with wood from responsibly managed sources, so as to minimise its environmental footprint.

10 9 8 7 6 5 4 3 2 1 24 25 26 27 28 / 2